For Magdalen
with love
S.H.

For Elaine Greene
with my love and appreciation
H.C.

First United States Edition 1990

Margaret K. McElderry Books
Macmillan Publishing Company
866 Third Avenue, New York, NY 10022

Text copyright © 1990 by Sarah Hayes
Illustrations copyright © 1990 by Helen Craig
First published by Walker Books Ltd., London

Printed in Hong Kong by South China Printing Co. (1988) Limited

10 9 8 7 6 5 4 3 2 1

CIP is available.

ISBN 0-689-50514-0

MARY MARY

WRITTEN BY SARAH HAYES

ILLUSTRATED BY HELEN CRAIG

Margaret K. McElderry Books
New York

There was once a little girl called Mary Mary. Her real name was Mary, but everyone called her Mary Mary because she was so contrary. It didn't matter what you said, Mary Mary always said something different. If you said yes, Mary Mary said no. If you said good, Mary Mary said terrible. If you said it was hot, Mary Mary said it was freezing. She was just plain contrary. Above the town where Mary Mary lived was a hill, and on top of the hill stood a huge house where a giant lived. The people in the town were terrified of the giant, and they ran away whenever they saw him. Not Mary Mary. She wasn't afraid of any old giant, or so she said. No one believed her.

One day Mary Mary set off to visit the giant. The other children followed her as far as they dared.

Mary Mary climbed right up to the top of the hill and onto the giant's huge doorstep. Then she began to bounce her ball against the door.

The great door opened suddenly. The other children screamed and ran away. Not Mary Mary. She stayed just where she was on the step.

Then something peculiar happened. An enormous splash of salty water suddenly landed on Mary Mary's head and knocked her clean off the step.

The next thing she knew, Mary Mary was flat on her back, wrapped in a sheet, staring at the ceiling. It seemed a very long way off. Mary Mary sat up and gave a little gasp. She saw that she was sitting in a giant matchbox on a giant table with the giant himself looking right at her. But she wasn't afraid. Well, not really. Not Mary Mary.

The giant spoke in a hoarse voice that sounded as if it hadn't been used much. "You're all right," he said.

"No, I'm not," said Mary Mary. "I ache all over." She climbed out of the box and took a good look at the giant. "Hm," she said, "you are big."

"I'm too big," said the giant.

"No, you're not," said Mary Mary. "You're a giant."

"Everyone's afraid of me," said the giant.

"No, they aren't," said Mary Mary. "I'm not."

The giant didn't believe her. Tears welled up in his eyes and began to roll down his cheeks. Mary Mary remembered the great salty splash that had knocked her off the step.

"And I'm a mess," sniffed the giant.

Mary Mary started to say, "No, you're not," but then she stopped. The giant was right. He was a mess. A dreadful mess. And so was his house. Mary Mary used her sheet, which she now saw to be an enormous handkerchief, to dry the giant's tears.

"You really aren't afraid of me?" asked the giant.

"No, I'm not," said Mary Mary.

"And I'm really not too big?"

"Not for a giant," said Mary Mary.

"But I am a mess?"

"Yes," agreed Mary Mary. "You're definitely a mess." She felt very odd. Not contrary at all. "What you need," she said firmly, "is managing."

And for the rest of the day Mary Mary managed the giant. First they did house managing: they tidied and washed and polished and sewed and glued and sorted. Then they did garden managing and raked and swept and clipped and weeded.

By that time they were both filthy, so the giant heated some water for baths. Mary Mary had her bath in a teacup. Then she and the giant sat down with pens and paper to do a last bit of managing.

Just before sunset Mary Mary climbed into the giant's waistcoat pocket, and the giant took her home. In his hand the giant held a large envelope.

When the people
in the town heard the
giant's footsteps come
whumping down the
hill, they all ran into
their houses and locked their doors. The Mayor hid
under his bed. Then the whumps went back up the
hill, and there was silence. People began to creep
back onto the streets. Then a shout went up – "It's
Mary Mary, and she's safe!" Everyone began to
crowd into the market square. There was Mary Mary
standing beside a huge envelope. And she was smiling.

The Mayor heard the noise of people shouting
and came out from under his bed.
He marched out onto the square.

"So you managed to escape
from the giant,"
he said.

"No, I didn't," said Mary Mary, "he brought me home."

"But he eats children for breakfast," said the Mayor.

"No, he doesn't," said Mary Mary, "he eats bread and jam for breakfast like everyone else, only bigger." But no one believed her. They thought she was just being contrary.

"Read the letter," said Mary Mary.

It took a few minutes to open the envelope and a few more minutes to unfold the paper and read the writing. This is what it said:

GRAND OPENING
TOMORROW
GIANT PLAYGROUND
HILL HOUSE
Wear old clothes
(Manager: Mary Mary)

The children forgot all about being frightened of the giant and began to look very excited.

"You can't go," said the Mayor.

"Yes, they can," said Mary Mary.

"Of course we can," said the children.

Very early next morning the children streamed up the hill toward the giant's house. The Mayor and the grown-ups followed as fast as they could. But when they arrived, wheezing and panting, at the top of the hill, the children were nowhere to be seen. The Mayor and the grown-ups rushed through the giant's open door, through the house and into the garden at the back. Then they stopped.

At first all they could see was children. Children sliding, children jumping, children swinging, children bouncing, children climbing. And then the grown-ups realized that underneath all the sliding, jumping, swinging, bouncing, climbing children lay the giant. Mary Mary was managing things from the top of a tall ladder.

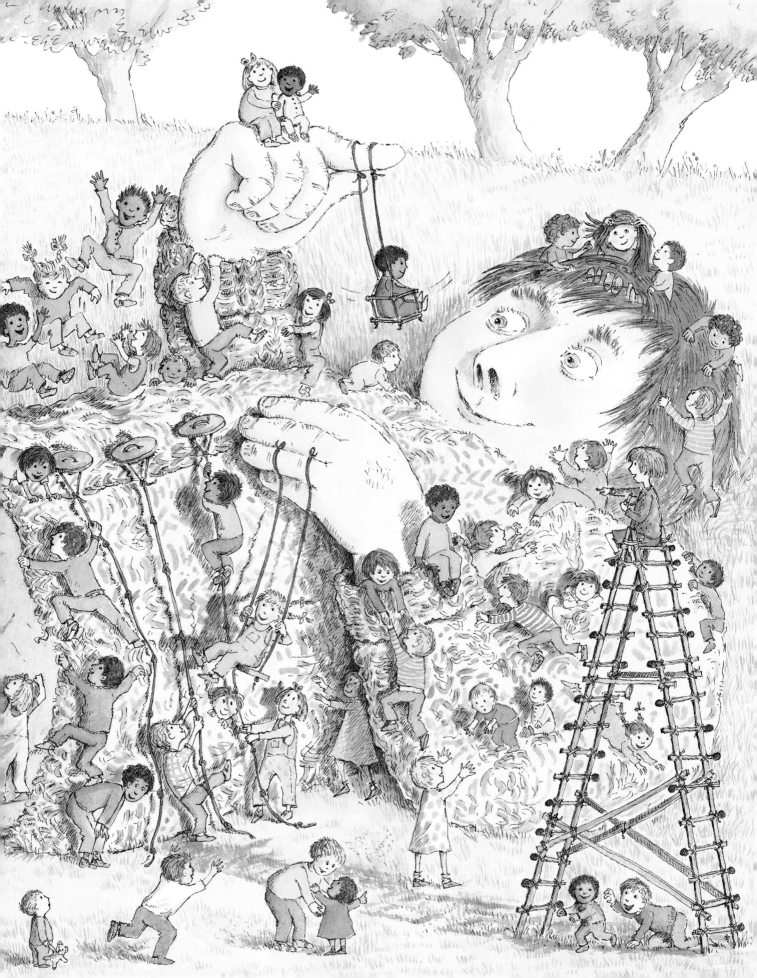

The Mayor marched up. "This playground is ridiculous," he said.

"No, it isn't," said Mary Mary quietly.

"This playground is dangerous," said the Mayor.

"No, it isn't," shouted the children.

"This playground is impossible," said the Mayor.

"No, it isn't," shouted Mary Mary, the children, and the grown-ups all together.

"Then I suppose I must declare this playground open," said the Mayor.

"Yes," said Mary Mary.

At the end of the day everyone walked back down the hill, chatting and laughing. All except Mary Mary. She stayed behind to talk to the giant on her own. He was very tired, but he was still smiling.

"Well," said Mary Mary, "we managed it."

"No, we didn't," said the giant. "You managed it."

"Yes," said Mary Mary, "I think I did."

THE END